Nonsense
Poems

North South Books

~

New York

~

London

THE OWL AND THE PUSSY~CAT

AND OTHER
NONSENSE
POEMS BY
EDWARD
LEAR

~

SELECTED AND
ILLUSTRATED BY
MICHAEL
HAGUE

To the owners and players of professional baseball,
who know more about nonsense than Mr. Lear or I will ever know. —M.H.

Published in the United States by North-South Books Inc., New York.
Published simultaneously in Great Britain, Canada, Australia, and
New Zealand in 1995 by North-South Books, an imprint of
Nord-Süd Verlag AG, Gossau Zürich, Switzerland.
Library of Congress Cataloging-in-Publication Data
Lear, Edward, 1812-1888.
The owl and the pussy-cat, and other nonsense poems /
by Edward Lear ; selected and illustrated by Michael Hague.
Summary: An illustrated collection of twenty-four
nonsensical poems by Edward Lear.
1. Children's poetry, English. 2. Nonsense verses, English.
[1. Nonsense verses. 2. English poetry.]
I. Michael Hague, ill. II. Title.
PR4879.L209 1995 821′.8—DC20 95-13076
A CIP catalogue record for this book
is available from The British Library.
Designed by Marc Cheshire
ISBN 1-55858-467-6 (trade edition)
TB 10 9 8 7 6 5 4 3 2
ISBN 1-55858-468-4 (library edition)
LB 10 9 8 7 6 5 4 3 2
Printed in Italy

Contents

Calico pie,
  The little Birds fly
Down to the calico-tree:
Their wings were blue,
And they sang "Tilly-loo!"
Till away they flew;
  And they never came back to me!
    They never came back,
    They never came back,
  They never came back to me!

Calico jam,
  The little Fish swam
Over the Syllabub Sea.
  He took off his hat
  To the Sole and the Sprat,
  And the Willeby-wat:
But he never came back to me;
  He never came back,
  He never came back,
He never came back to me.

Calico ban,
The little Mice ran
To be ready in time for tea;
Flippity flup,
They drank it all up,
And danced in the cup:
But they never came back to me;
They never came back,
They never came back,
They never came back to me.

Calico drum,
The Grasshoppers come,
The Butterfly, Beetle, and Bee,
Over the ground,
Around and round,
With a hop and a bound;
But they never came back
They never came back
They never came back
They never came back to me.

THERE WAS AN OLD MAN OF DUMBREE

~

There was an Old Man of Dumbree,
Who taught little owls to drink tea;
For he said, "To eat mice is not proper or nice,"
That amiable Man of Dumbree.

There was an Old Man in a Marsh,
Whose manners were futile and harsh;
He sate on a log, and sang songs to a frog,
That instructive Old Man in a Marsh.

THERE WAS
AN OLD MAN
IN A MARSH
~

A was an ant
Who seldom stood still,
And who made a nice house
In the side of a hill.
a
Nice little ant!

AN ALPHABET
~

B was a book
With a binding of blue,
And pictures and stories
For me and for you.
b
Nice little book!

C was a cat
Who ran after a rat;
But his courage did fail
When she seized on his tail.
c
Crafty old cat!

D was a duck
With spots on his back,
Who lived in the water,
And always said "Quack!"
d
Dear little duck!

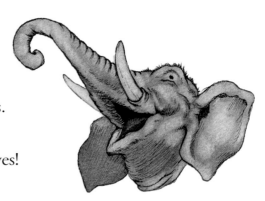

E was an elephant,
Stately and wise:
He had tusks and trunk,
And two queer little eyes.
e
Oh, what funny small eyes!

F was a fish
Who was caught in a net;
But he got out again,
And is quite alive yet.
f
Lively young fish!

G was a goat
Who was spotted with brown:
When he did not lie still
He walked up and down.
g
Good little goat!

H was a hat
Which was all on one side;
Its crown was too high,
And its brim was too wide.
h
Oh, what a hat!

I was some ice
So white and so nice,
But which nobody tasted;
And so it was wasted.
i
All that good ice!

J was a jackdaw
Who hopped up and down
In the principal street
Of a neighboring town.
j
All through the town!

K was a kite
Which flew out of sight,
Above houses so high,
Quite into the sky.
k
Fly away, kite!

L was a light
Which burned all the night,
And lighted the gloom
Of a very dark room.
l
Useful nice light!

M was a mill
Which stood on a hill,
And turned round and round
With a loud hummy sound.
m
Useful old mill!

N was a net
Which was thrown in the sea
To catch fish for dinner
For you and for me.
n
Nice little net!

O was an orange
So yellow and round:
When it fell off the tree,
It fell down to the ground.
o
Down to the ground!

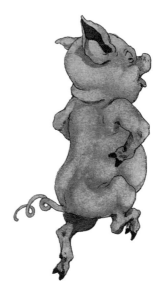

P was a pig,
Who was not very big;
But his tail was too curly,
And that made him surly.

p

Cross little pig!

Q was a quail
With a very short tail;
And he fed upon corn
In the evening and morn.

q

Quaint little quail!

R was a rabbit,
Who had a bad habit
Of eating the flowers
In gardens and bowers.

r

Naughty fat rabbit!

S was the sugar-tongs,
Nippity-nee,
To take up the sugar
To put in our tea.

s

Nippity-nee!

T was a tortoise,
All yellow and black:
He walked slowly away,
And he never came back.

t

Torty never came back!

U was an urn
All polished and bright,
And full of hot water
At noon and at night.
u
Useful old urn!

V was a villa
Which stood on a hill,
By the side of a river,
And close to a mill.
v
Nice little villa!

W was a whale
With a very long tail,
Whose movements were frantic
Across the Atlantic.
w
Monstrous old whale!

X was King Xerxes,
Who, more than all Turks, is
Renowned for his fashion
Of fury and passion.
x
Angry old Xerxes!

Y was a yew,
Which flourished and grew
By a quiet abode
Near the side of a road.
y
Dark little yew!

Z was some zinc,
So shiny and bright,
Which caused you to wink
In the sun's merry light.
Z
Beautiful zinc!

THERE WAS AN OLD MAN OF DUNLUCE
~

There was an Old Man of Dunluce,
Who went out to sea on a goose:
When he'd gone out a mile, he observ'd with a smile,
"It is time to return to Dunluce."

There was an Old Person of Bree,
Who frequented the depths of the sea;
She nurs'd the small fishes, and washed all the dishes,
And swam back again into Bree.

The Owl and the Pussy-Cat went to sea
 In a beautiful pea-green boat:
They took some honey, and plenty of money
 Wrapped up in a five-pound note.
The Owl looked up to the stars above,
 And sang to a small guitar,
"O lovely Pussy, O Pussy, my love,
 What a beautiful Pussy you are,
   You are,
   You are!
 What a beautiful Pussy you are!"

THE OWL AND THE PUSSY-CAT
~

Pussy said to the Owl, "You elegant fowl,
How charmingly sweet you sing!
Oh! let us be married; too long we have tarried:
But what shall we do for a ring?"
They sailed away, for a year and a day,
To the land where the bong-tree grows;
And there in a wood a Piggy-wig stood,
With a ring at the end of his nose,
His nose,
His nose,
With a ring at the end of his nose.

"Dear Pig, are you willing to sell for one shilling
    Your ring?" Said the Piggy, "I will."
So they took it away, and were married next day
    By the Turkey who lives on the hill.
They dined on mince and slices of quince,
    Which they ate with a runcible spoon;
And hand in hand, on the edge of the sand,
    They danced by the light of the moon,
            The moon,
            The moon,
    They danced by the light of the moon.

THERE WAS A YOUNG LADY iN WHITE
~

There was a Young Lady in White,
Who looked out at the depths of the night;
But the birds of the air, filled her heart with despair,
And oppressed that Young Lady in White.

There was an Old Person of Hove,
Who frequented the depths of a grove;
Where he studied his books, with the wrens and the rooks,
That tranquil Old Person of Hove.

THERE WAS AN
OLD PERSON
OF HOVE
~

THERE WAS AN OLD PERSON OF WARE
~

There was an Old Person of Ware,
Who rode on the back of a bear;
When they ask'd, "Does it trot?" he said, "Certainly not!
He's a Moppsikon Floppsikon bear!"

There was an Old Lady of France,
Who taught little ducklings to dance;
When she said, "Tick-a-Tack!" they only said, "Quack!"
Which grieved that Old Lady of France.

THERE WAS
AN OLD LADY
OF FRANCE
~

THERE WAS AN OLD MAN OF BOULAK
~

There was an Old Man of Boulak,
Who sate on a Crocodile's back;
But they said, "Tow'rds the night he may probably bite,
Which might vex you, Old Man of Boulak!"

There is a Young Lady, whose nose,
Continually prospers and grows;
When it grew out of sight, she exclaimed in a fright,
"Oh! Farewell to the end of my nose!"

The Cummerbund

~

an Indian Poem

~

I.

She sate upon her Dobie,

    To watch the Evening Star,

And all the Punkahs, as they passed,

    Cried, "My! how fair you are!"

Around her bower, with quivering leaves,

    The tall Kamsamahs grew,

And Kitmutgars in wild festoons

    Hung down from Tchokis blue.

II.

Below her home the river rolled
    With soft meloobious sound,
Where golden-finned Chuprassies swam,
    In myriads circling round.
Above, on tallest trees remote
    Green Ayahs perched alone,
And all night long the Mussak moan'd
    Its melancholy tone.

III.

And where the purple Nullahs threw
    Their branches far and wide,
And silvery Goreewallahs flew
    In silence, side by side,
The little Bheesties' twittering cry
    Rose on the flagrant air,
And oft the angry Jampan howled
    Deep in his hateful lair.

IV.

She sate upon her Dobie,
   She heard the Nimmak hum,
When all at once a cry arose,
   "The Cummerbund is come!"
In vain she fled: with open jaws
   The angry monster followed,
And so (before assistance came)
   That Lady Fair was swollowed.

V.

They sought in vain for even a bone
    Respectfully to bury;
They said, "Hers was a dreadful fate!"
    (And Echo answered, "Very.")
They nailed her Dobie to the wall,
    Where last her form was seen,
And underneath they wrote these words,
    In yellow, blue, and green:

"Beware, ye Fair! Ye Fair, beware!
    Nor sit out late at night,
Lest horrid Cummerbunds should come,
    And swollow you outright."

There was a Young Lady whose eyes
Were unique as to color and size;
When she opened them wide, people all turned aside,
And started away in surprise.

THERE WAS
A YOUNG LADY
WHOSE EYES
~

**THERE WAS
AN OLD MAN
OF LEGHORN**
~

There was an Old Man of Leghorn,
The smallest that ever was born;
But quickly snapt up he was once by a Puppy,
Who devoured that Old Man of Leghorn.

There was a Young Lady of Portugal,
Whose ideas were excessively nautical;
She climbed up a tree to examine the sea,
But declared she would never leave Portugal.

THERE WAS
A YOUNG LADY
OF PORTUGAL
~

THERE WAS A YOUNG LADY OF BUTE
~

There was a Young Lady of Bute,
Who played on a silver-gilt flute;
She played several jigs to her Uncle's white Pigs:
That amusing Young Lady of Bute.

There was an Old Man who said, "Hush!
I perceive a young bird in this bush!"
When they said, "Is it small?" he replied, "Not at all;
It is four times as big as the bush!"

THERE WAS AN
OLD MAN WHO
SAID, "HUSH!"
~

THE COURTSHIP OF THE YONGHY~ BONGHY~BÒ

I.

On the Coast of Coromandel
    Where the early pumpkins blow,
      In the middle of the woods
    Lived the Yonghy-Bonghy-Bò.
Two old chairs, and half a candle,
One old jug without a handle,—
    These were all his worldly goods:
      In the middle of the woods,
      These were all the worldly goods
    Of the Yonghy-Bonghy-Bò,
    Of the Yonghy-Bonghy-Bò.

II.

Once, among the Bong-trees walking
    Where the early pumpkins blow,
        To a little heap of stones
    Came the Yonghy-Bonghy-Bò.
There he heard a Lady talking,
To some milk-white Hens of Dorking,—
           "'Tis the Lady Jingly Jones!
          On that little heap of stones
          Sits the Lady Jingly Jones!"
        Said the Yonghy-Bonghy-Bò,
        Said the Yonghy-Bonghy-Bò.

III.

"Lady Jingly! Lady Jingly!

    Sitting where the pumpkins blow,

        Will you come and be my wife?"

    Said the Yonghy-Bonghy-Bò.

"I am tired of living singly,—

On this coast so wild and shingly,—

        I'm a-weary of my life;

        If you'll come and be my wife,

        Quite serene would be my life!"

    Said the Yonghy-Bonghy-Bò,

    Said the Yonghy-Bonghy-Bò.

IV.

"On this Coast of Coromandel

    Shrimps and watercresses grow,

        Prawns are plentiful and cheap,"

    Said the Yonghy-Bonghy-Bò.

"You shall have my chairs and candle,

And my jug without a handle!

        Gaze upon the rolling deep

        (Fish is plentiful and cheap);

        As the sea, my love is deep!"

    Said the Yonghy-Bonghy-Bò,

    Said the Yonghy-Bonghy-Bò.

V.

Lady Jingly answered sadly,

    And her tears began to flow,—

        "Your proposal comes too late,

    Mr. Yonghy-Bonghy-Bò!

I would be your wife most gladly!"

(Here she twirled her fingers madly.)

        "But in England I've a mate!

        Yes! you've asked me far too late,

        For in England I've a mate,

Mr. Yonghy-Bonghy-Bò!

Mr. Yonghy-Bonghy-Bò!

VI.

"Mr. Jones (his name is Handel,—
    Handel Jones, Esquire, & Co.)
        Dorking fowls delights to send,
    Mr. Yonghy-Bonghy-Bò!
Keep, oh, keep your chairs and candle,
And your jug without a handle,—
        I can merely be your friend!
        Should my Jones more Dorkings send,
        I will give you three, my friend!
    Mr. Yonghy-Bonghy-Bò!
    Mr. Yonghy-Bonghy-Bò!

VII.

"Though you've such a tiny body,
    And your head so large doth grow,—
        Though your hat may blow away,
    Mr. Yonghy-Bonghy-Bò!
Though you're such a Hoddy Doddy,
Yet I wish that I could modi-
        fy the words I needs must say!
        Will you please to go away?
        That is all I have to say,
    Mr. Yonghy-Bonghy-Bò!
    Mr. Yonghy-Bonghy-Bò!"

VIII.

Down the slippery slopes of Myrtle,
    Where the early pumpkins blow,
        To the calm and silent sea
    Fled the Yonghy-Bonghy-Bò.
There, beyond the Bay of Gurtle,
Lay a large and lively Turtle.
        "You're the Cove," he said, "for me;
            On your back beyond the sea,
            Turtle, you shall carry me!"
    Said the Yonghy-Bonghy-Bò,
    Said the Yonghy-Bonghy-Bò.

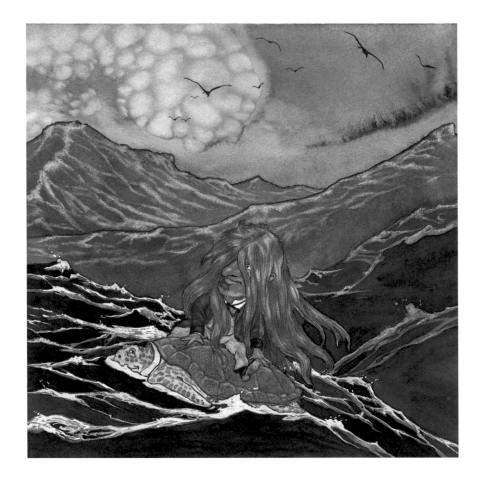

IX.
Through the silent-roaring ocean
    Did the Turtle swiftly go;
       Holding fast upon his shell
    Rode the Yonghy-Bonghy-Bò.
With a sad primæval motion
Towards the sunset isles of Boshen
       Still the Turtle bore him well.
       Holding fast upon his shell,
        "Lady Jingly Jones, farewell!"
    Sang the Yonghy-Bonghy-Bò,
    Sang the Yonghy-Bonghy-Bò.

X.

From the Coast of Coromandel
    Did that Lady never go;
        On that heap of stones she mourns
    For the Yonghy-Bonghy-Bò.
On that Coast of Coromandel
In his jug without a handle
        Still she weeps, and daily moans;
        On that little heap of stones
        To her Dorking Hens she moans,
    For the Yonghy-Bonghy-Bò,
    For the Yonghy-Bonghy-Bò.

THERE WAS AN OLD PERSON OF HYDE

~

There was an Old Person of Hyde,
Who walked by the shore with his bride,
Till a Crab who came near fill'd their bosoms with fear,
And they said, "Would we'd never left Hyde!"

There was a Young Lady of Firle,
Whose hair was addicted to curl;
It curled up a tree, and all over the sea,
That expansive Young Lady of Firle.

THERE WAS
A YOUNG LADY
OF FIRLE
~

The Duck and the Kangaroo

I.

Said the Duck to the Kangaroo,

"Good gracious! how you hop

Over the fields, and the water too,

As if you never would stop!

My life is a bore in this nasty pond;

And I long to go out in the world beyond:

I wish I could hop like you,"

Said the Duck to the Kangaroo.

II.

"Please give me a ride on your back,"
    Said the Duck to the Kangaroo:
"I would sit quite still, and say nothing but 'Quack'
    The whole of the long day through;
And we'd go the Dee, and the Jelly Bo Lee,
Over the land, and over the sea:
    Please take me a ride! oh, do!"
    Said the Duck to the Kangaroo.

III.

Said the Kangaroo to the Duck,
    "This requires some little reflection.
Perhaps, on the whole, it might bring me luck:
    And there seems but one objection;
Which is, if you'll let me speak so bold,
Your feet are unpleasantly wet and cold,
    And would probably give me the roo-
    Matiz," said the Kangaroo.

IV.

Said the Duck, "As I sate on the rocks,
    I have thought over that completely;
And I bought four pairs of worsted socks,
    Which fit my web-feet neatly;
And, to keep out the cold, I've bought a cloak;
And every day a cigar I'll smoke;
    All to follow my own dear true
    Love of a Kangaroo."

V.

Said the Kangaroo, "I'm ready,
    All in the moonlight pale;
But to balance me well, dear Duck, sit steady.
    And quite at the end of my tail."
So away they went with a hop and a bound;
And they hopped the whole world three times round.
    And who so happy, oh! who,
    As the Duck and the Kangaroo?

There was an Old Man of the Hague,
Whose ideas were excessively vague;
He built a balloon to examine the moon,
That deluded Old Man of the Hague.